Books by Gladys Yessayan Cretan

A GIFT FROM THE BRIDE

ALL EXCEPT SAMMY

ALL EXCEPT SAMMY

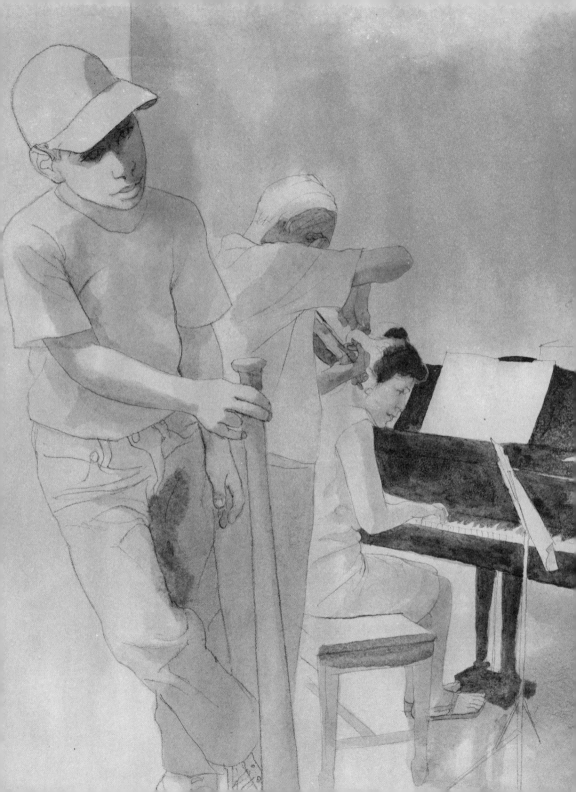

ALL EXCEPT SAMMY

by Gladys Yessayan Cretan

Illustrated by Symeon Shimin

An Atlantic Monthly Press Book

BOSTON   TORONTO   Little, Brown and Company

ATLANTIC-LITTLE, BROWN BOOKS
ARE PUBLISHED BY
LITTLE, BROWN AND COMPANY
IN ASSOCIATION WITH
THE ATLANTIC MONTHLY PRESS

Published simultaneously in Canada
by Little, Brown & Company (Canada) Limited

PRINTED IN THE UNITED STATES OF AMERICA

For Clifford and Larry—
my favorite baseball players

U. S. 1365421

EVERYONE in Sammy Agabashian's family was musical—except Sammy.

Mama played the piano.

Brother Armen played the clarinet.

Sister Lucy played the cello.

Papa played the violin, and was the conductor of a whole symphony orchestra.

Sammy played baseball.

3

Sometimes the family gave a concert together. They played sonatas and mazurkas and minuets. Usually Papa and Armen performed a duet especially written for violin and clarinet. Mama and Lucy always looked beautiful up on the stage in their long silk dresses.

Sammy sat in the audience and listened with the others.

When Armen played in his own recitals, or Lucy in hers, Sammy sat in front and clapped proudly along with Papa. Sometimes the people around them shouted "Bravo!" and Mama smiled happily.

Everyone said, "Such a talented family. All so musical."

Of course they meant everyone was talented but Sammy.

One day a man from the newspaper came to take a picture of these musical Agabashians. He grouped them all around the piano.

4

Mama sat at the piano bench, with her music spread in front of her. Armen stood next to her with his clarinet, ready to play. Lucy sat with her cello, the bow in position, and Papa was a little to the side with his baton raised.

Then the photographer turned to Sammy. "And what do you play?" he asked.

"Baseball," said Sammy.

"That's a good game, but I can't put you in this picture," said the man. "This is a picture of a musical family."

So while the picture was taken Sammy sat and watched.

Afterward he said to his mother, "I sure would like to be in the next family picture. What instrument could I learn?"

"We could use another violinist," his mother said. "We'll ask Papa to give you lessons."

Papa tried.

And Sammy tried.

But it never did sound right. In fact, it sounded horrible. When Sammy was playing, the cat scratched on the door to be let out, and the dog hid under the bed and howled. Even Sammy's best friend, Jason, quietly rolled his eyes and went home.

"Sammy," said his father, "even for a beginner this is terrible."

"Let's try the piano," said his mother, "and work on your rhythm."

For days and days they worked, and Sammy tried hard.

"Oh dear," said his sister Lucy.

"Something's wrong," said his brother Armen.

"*Hereek!* Enough!" said his father. "Mama, the boy has no rhythm. Absolutely no rhythm."

"Try again, Sammy," said his mother. "Listen now. One-and-two-and—no, no, no, Sammy. Can't you hear the beat?"

She sat back and shook her head. *"Vagh!"* she said. "I'm afraid your father is right."

Then she had another thought. "Perhaps he will be our singer. And someday he will sing arias. Come, Sammy, what would you like to sing?"

"Take Me Out to the Ball Game," said Sammy happily.

"All right," said his mother, and she started to play it on the piano. "Come," she said. "Sing out, Sammy."

And Sammy tried. He knew all the words. He sang the very best he could, and loud.

They all listened. And they all shook their heads.

"Tone-deaf," said his father. "He can't sing a note."

"How can this happen in this family?" said his mother. "Can the fruit fall so far from the tree?"

10

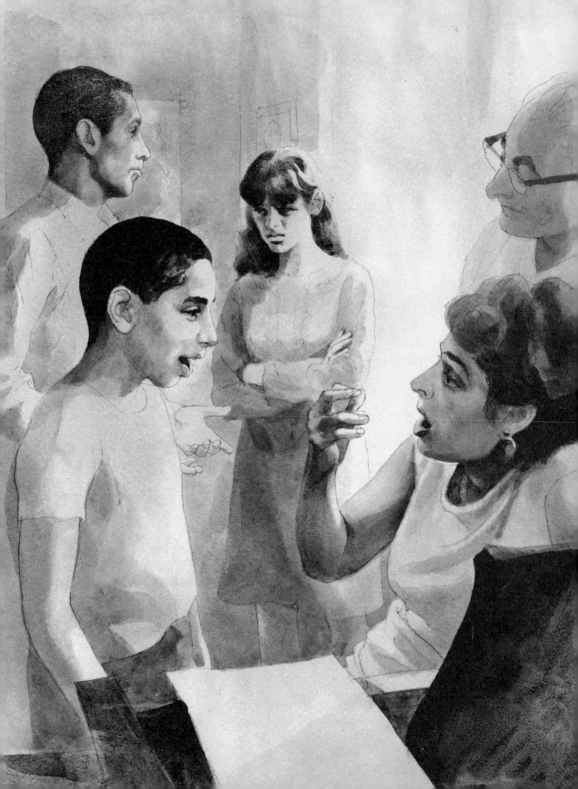

"Mama," said his father, "stop trying. It is like baking a stone. Nothing will come of it."

"Don't feel bad, Sammy," said his sister. "It doesn't matter."

"Who's feeling bad?" said Sammy.

"Come on," said his brother, "let's go out and play ball."

"Who cares about music anyway," said Sammy.

But Sammy really did want to be in a family picture.

After school the next day Sammy dashed home and ran upstairs to get his baseball bat and his mitt.

"There is a thunder in our house," said his mother.

"A thunder called Sammy," said his father, as Sammy rumbled down the stairs. "And look at that black cloud on his face. Why do you frown?"

12

"You'd frown too," said Sammy, "if you had to go to the museum."

"No," said his mother, "I often go, and it makes me happy. But why do you suddenly want to go to the museum?"

"Who wants to go?" said Sammy. "It's our homework. This week everybody has to go to the museum and find a favorite picture and tell about it."

"A good idea," said Papa.

"Listen," said Sammy, "I don't know anything about paintings. I don't even like them. How can I have a favorite?"

"Try," said his mother. "Slow down once and really look."

"One question," said his father. "Why the baseball bat?"

"Gosh," said Sammy, "I can't stay all day at the museum. I have baseball practice. And we're up for the championship."

14

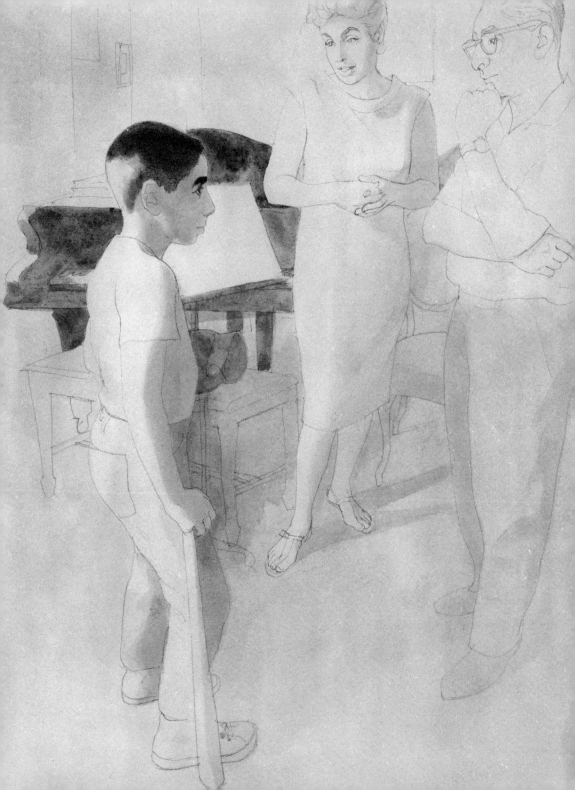

He walked slowly to the museum, hitting each telephone pole with his bat. At the big gray building with the tall columns in front he stopped and wondered.

He hadn't ever gone in before.

He walked up the wide stone steps and when he came to the great doorway he stopped again. He felt small.

When he stepped into the large center room with its statues and its curving stairs and its cool marble walls he looked around slowly. His footsteps were very loud. A museum guard came up to him and told him he would have to check his bat in the lobby.

Then he climbed the stairs and wandered through the bright rooms. There were paintings of sunflowers, of children dressed in blue velvet, of dancers, pink on white.

Sammy shrugged and gave his mitt a punch.

"Pictures for girls," he said.

He passed a picture of a stately medieval castle, of a golden-haired family, of a bowl of fruit shining in the sunlight. He shook his head.

When he saw a sparkling picture of small boats sailing he paused. That was better. But after a moment he walked on, wondering if he ever would find a real favorite.

He came back up the stairs and that was when he saw the painting of a brilliantly plumed soldier sitting tall on a proud black horse.

"There!" he said. "There's a picture a fellow could talk about." And he stopped and looked at it for a long time.

Across the quietness a voice said, "Hi, Sammy!" and Sammy turned to see his friend Jason standing in front of a large picture of the sea.

"Hi!" said Sammy. "Find your picture?"

"I guess I like this one," said Jason. "Looks like a big storm. What about you?"

"I'll tell about this one," Sammy said. "But we'd better go now. We're late, and they can't start that game without us."

The next day Sammy told his class about the picture.

"And that horse could gallop, or trot, or run like the wind," Sammy said.

Jason looked puzzled.

"Say!" he said later. "How could you tell how that horse could run?"

"You could see it in the picture!" said Sammy.

"Now look," said Jason, "I saw that picture, and I didn't see anything like that. And you even said that he had led a battalion parade!"

"I could tell that partly from the trappings he was wearing and partly from the proud way he held his head," Sammy answered. "Listen,

if you don't believe me, we'll stop there today on the way to the ball park and I'll show you."

"All right," said Jason, "but man," he rolled his eyes, "gallop and trot?"

"Look," said Sammy after school, as they stood in front of the picture. "Look at the power in that horse. Look at his smooth muscles. You mean to tell me that horse can't run? And see how the soldier is holding the reins. He's sure of that horse. He knows he can do anything!"

After a long look, Jason shook his head. "That's a lot to tell from a painting," he said.

Sammy nodded. "It's a lot for someone to show, just with a little paint," he said.

Jason moved slowly on around the large room. But Sammy sat on a bench and kept looking at the same picture. Jason tried walking in a circle on his heels. He swung his mitt around and around and went downstairs for a drink of water. He whistled between his teeth. When he came back Sammy still wasn't ready to go.

Jason scuffled his feet and waited and waited. "Didn't you see enough?" he asked at last.

"Look at this," Sammy answered.

"Same old picture," said Jason.

"I've been looking at the soldier's cape," said Sammy. "It's supposed to be red."

"Sure is red," Jason said. "Bright red."

"Yes," said Sammy, "when I first saw it I thought it was plain red. But I've really been looking at it. And I see that when you're close up to it, part of it is orange, part of it is almost black and part of it is white. But when you back away from it, it all comes out red."

Jason nodded. "I suppose an artist knows how to do that," he said.

"I'd like to know how to do it too," Sammy said. "Look how he used the white and the dark to make it look like folds in the cape. Listen, that's harder to figure out than any puzzle. I'll have to come back tomorrow to look at that some more."

24

Jason groaned. "More?" he said.

But Sammy wasn't listening. He was pointing to a sign. It was near the entrance, and it said there was a painting class for school children on Saturday mornings.

"Look!" Sammy said. "That's for me."

"Good," said Jason. "You can ask about that red coloring. I sure was getting tired of studying it."

They walked down the wide steps and turned toward the ball field, and Jason thought of something else.

"Hey!" he said. "Sammy! What about Saturday practice?"

"I'll only be a little late," Sammy said. "I wouldn't miss that."

"Sure," said Jason, "but what about Tug Smith?"

"Look," said Sammy. "We decided in the try-outs. I'm first base, and he's my substitute."

26

"I know," said Jason, "but if you don't come on Saturdays...Oh, oh, look. He's already standing there as if he owns first base."

Across the field they could see Tug standing with one foot on either side of first base. When he saw them cutting across the field he folded his arms and pulled himself up tall.

"He's not planning to move," said Jason.

"Too bad," said Sammy. "Hi, Tug."

"Hi," said Tug. "They need someone in left field."

"Good," said Sammy. "Then you can still play."

"Not me," said Tug. "I'm first base."

"Since when?" said Sammy.

"Since you were late twice in a row," said Tug.

"Listen," said Sammy. "I have to be late every Saturday, and you're my sub, fair enough, but I was chosen first base, and I'll be here as fast as I can."

28

"How come you'll be late?" asked Tug.

Sammy hesitated. "I have to take a class," he said.

"No school on Saturday," said Tug.

"I know," Sammy said. "This is a special class. Art. At the museum."

"Art?" hooted Tug. "Art? Hooo-eeee! Hey, fellas, he's going to be a painter."

"Cut it out!" said Sammy. "And get off that base."

"Make me get off, painter," laughed Tug. "Hooo-eeee!" And he doubled over.

Sammy stepped toward him with his fists up and his head down.

"Fight! Fight!" said the pitcher.

"Get him! Get him!" said the catcher.

"I'll hold your things, Sammy," said Jason.

"Put up your fists!" said the shortstop.

Tug laughed again, and leaned down to slap his leg. Sammy jumped. Over they rolled. And

over again. Arms and legs waved free, then were pinned down again. Under and over.

"Pin him down!" called the pitcher.

"Jackknife!" yelled the catcher.

"Yea!" called the shortstop.

Under again, and over they went. Dust flew. A shirt tore.

Suddenly Sammy was on top and had Tug pinned down. He wiped his forehead with his arm and he frowned down at Tug.

Everybody was quiet.

"Sammy," said Jason softly. "Don't hit him."

"Aw," said Sammy. "What's the matter with you guys? Why would I hurt him? He's even on our own team."

Then he looked back down at Tug.

"Listen," he said. "You're so smart. Can you paint a brown-black horse that looks like he can really run?"

Tug shook his head.

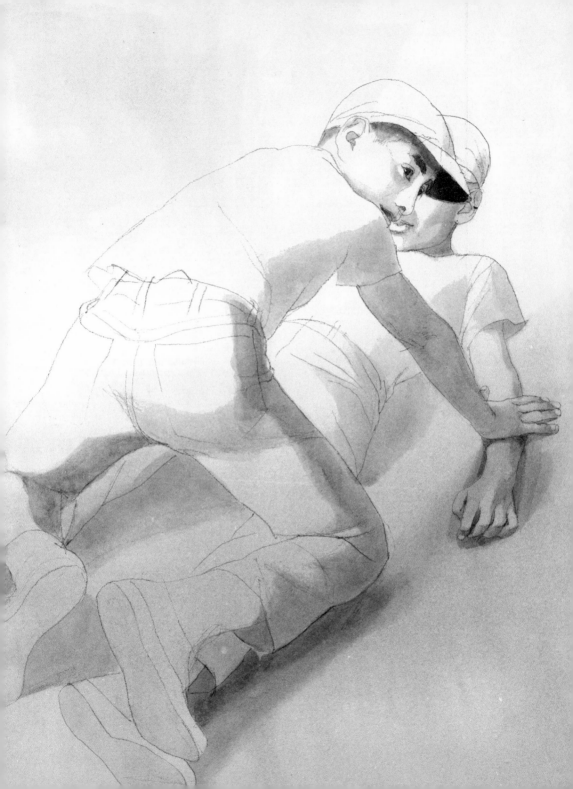

"Okay, and can you paint a storm at sea, or can you use orange and gray and white, and still have a cape look red?"

Tug said no.

"Neither can I," said Sammy, "but that's what I'm going to try to learn. And it's tough. Just as tough as playing baseball. See?"

Tug nodded, and as they both stood up and dusted themselves off, Sammy continued, "So I'll be a little late on Saturdays, and you can sub. Right?"

"Well," said Tug. He looked over to first base. Then he looked at all the faces around him, and back to Sammy. "Well, all right," he said.

So every Saturday, while Mama gave piano lessons downstairs, and Armen and Lucy practiced their instruments upstairs, and Papa went to rehearse his orchestra, Sammy went to the art class.

"What about the baseball team?" Papa asked

as he walked one morning with Sammy toward the museum.

"I get there a little late," Sammy said, "but the fellows don't mind because I'm painting a poster for them. We'll be the only team with our own special colors and our own poster to put up whenever we're playing."

"They're lucky to have an artist on the team," said Papa. "Look at the trouble we have getting our program covers designed. And our posters for the front of the concert hall. *Agh!* Either they look like a grocery list or they look like circus posters! A musician needs a musical poster. Ah, well. Here's the museum. Learn well!"

When Jason arrived later, Sammy was sitting quietly in front of a picture of a little girl, looking, looking.

"Studying something new?" asked Jason.

"Blue," said Sammy. "This week I'm studying blue for a new painting I started. Look," he pointed, "look at that blue dress. Part green, and part black, but it all comes out blue."

"That's a fact," said Jason. "Never saw it that way before."

He picked up Sammy's mitt and gave it a punch. "We get to use the big field today," he said. "Can you play late?"

"Sure," said Sammy. "There's no use going home early today, anyway. There's a man coming to take a picture of the family."

"You're in the family," said Jason.

"I know," said Sammy, "but he only wants the musicians in the family. All but me."

"Never mind, Sammy," said Jason. "Maybe you can't fiddle but you sure can draw."

"That's true," said Sammy. "I can draw. And I've been thinking. Why can't I design the program cover for their concert. And I'll bet I could plan a good poster. I could paint the instruments that they play...maybe in blue like in this picture..."

38

Sammy worked hard. He worked for days and days. Sometimes he painted at the museum, and sometimes at home. While he worked he would hum, "Take me out to the ball game..."

"*Vagh,*" said Mama under her breath, when she heard him.

"Tone-deaf," said Papa, shaking his head.

But one day Armen called, "Look! Look at Sammy's poster!"

And Lucy said, "Why this is better than any poster we've ever had."

And it was.

So this time when the photographer came he put Sammy right in the middle of the family, holding his poster. And when the picture of all the Agabashians appeared in the newspaper they were called "An Artistic Family."

"Boy!" said Sammy. "Look at that! I finally got in the picture."

"And why not?" said his father. "Must every-

one play an instrument? No. You are an artist. And a good one!"

"Not only that," said Armen, "he's a good ball player."

"Championship game tomorrow," said Lucy.

"We'll be there," said Papa Agabashian. "All of us."

And the next day, there they were, sitting on the bleachers, cheering the team. There were all the talented Agabashians — except Sammy.

Sammy was at home plate, swinging his bat, waiting for the pitch. When he felt the crack of his bat against the ball he ran, ran, safe to first base!

He heard the yells and the whistles of the crowd. He heard the clapping and shouting of Jason and the team. He heard his family calling, "Bravo!"

"Sounds like music to me!" he said.

Little Wu, who lives in the Village Facing the Sun, loves his mother very much. As he rides his water buffalo to the pasture he often dreams of earning money to buy her a silver ornament. But Mama and Baba have a bigger dream. They want to save enough money to buy a field of their own. They work hard and save every coin. But, alas, there is not enough money to buy the field. You will want to discover how Little Wu finds a secret way to earn money, and what he does with it. *Winner of the 1954 Charles W. Follett Award.*

Little Wu and the Watermelons

THE
Charles W. Follett Award

PRESENTED ANNUALLY

FOR WORTHY CONTRIBUTIONS
TO CHILDREN'S LITERATURE

Little Wu and the Watermelons

by Beatrice Liu

Illustrations by GRAHAM PECK

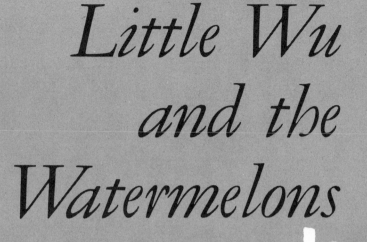

小吳與西瓜。

Follett Publishing Company

CHICAGO   NEW YORK   TORONTO

Foreword

Little Wu is not a Chinese, but a member of one of the many old tribes that live in Southwest China. These are descendants of people who were there before the Chinese came, just as the Indians were in America before the white people.

Little Wu lived in The Village Facing the Sun (Ch'ao Yang Ch'ün), near the market place of Flowery River (Hua Ch'i), about thirteen miles south of the city of Kweiyang, capital of Kweichow province. He belonged to the Flowery Miao (Hua Miao) tribe. Other Hua Miao people, only a short distance away, might have quite different clothing and customs.

In Hua Ch'i, Chinese and Miao people have lived close together for so long that their customs are mixed up, and the Miao often speak Chinese even among themselves. Since modern roads have been built and many outsiders are coming into the region, the tribal customs may soon nearly disappear.

The time of the story is 1942, during the war between China and Japan. Many people from the coastal regions of China, which had been taken by the Japanese, had come as refugees to the free provinces near Tibet. They were called "down-river people." They brought many new things, including the watermelons which are so important to our story. Watermelons are called "western melons" in Chinese, because they came from Chinese Turkestan, west of China.

As a result of the war, China was having a very bad inflation. That means that the value of the paper money was going down all the time, so that if you had enough money to buy a field and you kept it in paper money for a few months, it might be just enough to buy a watermelon. That is why, when people wanted to save money, they had to change it into silver dollars or pieces of gold.

Not all the people whom Little Wu calls "Uncle" or "Auntie" are related to him. It is polite for him to address all the friends of his parents this way.

Hua Ch'i is the loveliest place I have ever lived in. My window in The Village Facing the Sun looked across a rice field to the path where Little Wu rode the buffalo to pasture.

Beatrice Liu

Mound, Minnesota
May 24, 1954

To my husband,
who led me to
The Village Facing the Sun

LITTLE WU was thinking hard as he rode his father's buffalo across the road, through the woods, and up the twisting path among the rice fields to the pasture on the mountainside.

How could he buy a bracelet for his mother? The question had been in his mind ever since his return from market the day before.

小吳與西瓜

At market he had seen Third Wang and his father choosing a beaten brass bracelet of delicate design. When he asked what it was for, Third Wang had said, "It is for my mother, because she is the most beautiful mother in the world."

Until then, Little Wu had never thought much about the ornaments that were sold on market day, nor about whether women were beautiful or not. His own mother had no jewelry. In his family money was scarce, and seldom spent for anything. It had never occurred to him that a beautiful mother needed any ornament.

He thought it over as he walked around the market place. There was Third Wang's mother laughing and joking with the men who crowded around to buy her fried onion cakes from the broad black griddle. She had a large silver ring around her neck and a handsomely embroidered cloth hanging from her shoulders. Her pleated dark blue hempen kilt was almost new, better than the one Little Wu's mother wore to dances. She looked very gay, but as for beauty, well . . .

Little Wu walked on to where his own mother sat behind her trays of bean cheese. He looked at her hard. She seldom wore the tribal kilt except on festival days. Now, as usual, she was dressed in the simple blue trousers and jacket

of a Chinese farm woman, faded, but very clean. Her hair was combed back smoothly and coiled at the back of her head. She had small features for a Miao woman, and her dark skin glowed with health.

It was a pleasure to watch the graceful movements of her strong hands as she slipped a knife under a square of bean cheese, placed it on a clean dried lotus leaf, and handed it to a customer. Then her eyes fell on her son, and lit up in a smile.

"There you are!" she said. "Will you go and see whether Baba has sold the pheasant? Tell him I am nearly ready to go home."

Surely, thought the boy, she is more beautiful than Auntie Wang. I ought to buy her a bracelet to show that I think so.

But how could he do it? Baba and Mama were poor. They had worked and saved a long time to buy the young buffalo, which was still not old enough to plow a field. Baba had no fields of his own, but he worked hard, planting other men's land and receiving part of what he raised for his own share.

The house where they lived, in The Village Facing the Sun, was just a framework of poles, well thatched, with walls of woven straw. The floor was of packed earth with lime beaten into it. The buffalo shed and pig sty were built against the north wall outside to protect it a little in winter. Not much of a house, but it would do until they could buy materials to build a better one. What was life good for, Baba often asked, if people couldn't be always planning for something?

In this flimsy dwelling they already had most of what they really needed for daily life: solid wooden beds with clean quilts folded neatly on them, two good chests, a crude table and benches that Baba had made himself, and a clay stove, besides the farming tools and kitchen utensils.

When Baba had free time, he always sat down and wove straw sandals or mattresses to sell, or carried thorn bushes from the mountains to build fences for his neighbors.

Mama worked hard too. She ground her own soybeans to make milk for the family and cheese to sell on market day. She wrapped her hands with rags while she cut hot, wild sting-nettles to spin and weave into coarse linen for the family's clothes. She fed the bean residue and rice washings to a pig and went out on the mountains to gather green stuff, which she boiled and poured in the feeding tub to make the pork firm and sweet. When Baba was lucky enough to catch a wild pheasant in his traps, Mama would keep it in a bamboo cage and feed it steamed grain until it could be sold for almost the price of a chicken.

Even when Mama was walking anywhere, her hands were busy twisting fibers of fine hemp into a smooth thread which she would boil in lime until it was soft and glossy and sell for embroidery floss or for stitching quilt covers.

Baba often said that with such a wife, he wouldn't stay poor long. He planned that by the time the buffalo was old enough to pull a plow, he would be able to buy a little field to plow with it. Then the crop would be all his own and he could more easily save money to buy another field, until he would have enough for all his family's needs.

If Little Wu wanted to buy his mother a present, he would have to earn the money all himself, and even without his parents' knowledge. If they knew he had money, they would ask him to put it into Baba's pocket. As soon as Baba had enough, he would buy a silver dollar and put it into the gourd bank in which they were saving their money to buy the field.

Little Wu thought and thought as the young buffalo, which they had named Head One because they hoped to have more some day, walked with slow, rocking steps. At last it reached a grassy slope where several brown cows and gray buffalo were grazing. Rich neighbor Ying had come himself with his six head of cattle. He sat on a rock, braiding a straw sandal. When Little Wu slid off Head One beside him, Old Ying looked up with a smile.

"You are a clever boy," he said, "and I see that you take good care of that little beast. I wonder, now, if you would

know how to bring back that stubborn old fellow of mine
that has strayed to the top of the hill."

"That's easy," cried Little Wu, and ran around to
approach the big buffalo from the other side. The beast

looked up, snorted, and did not move, but when Little Wu twisted his tail slightly, he lumbered down the hill.

"Well done," said Old Ying as Little Wu returned. "Now, little boy, listen carefully. I have brought these cattle of mine to pasture myself through the winter, since my son is in school and I have no one to help me at home. Now spring is coming, and I shall soon need all my time in the fields. I need someone like you to help me. You have to bring your own beast out anyway, so it will be no great thing for you to come by my house and take them all together. If you take good care of them and keep them fat and healthy, I will give you as much rice as you can carry at harvest time."

Little Wu was excited. He promised eagerly. This was his chance to earn something. Then he remembered that any such earnings would belong to the family and would go to the gourd bank. Well, that was good too. He would be proud to help buy the field that would provide a better living for all the family, even though it did not solve the problem of the bracelet. Little Wu thought of something else.

"Uncle Ying," he said, "it must often happen, since your son is in school, that you need the help of someone like me to save your time for more important work. I will be glad to do whatever jobs you offer me."

"I will not forget," said Old Ying. "You are a good boy, and there is much to do on a place like mine."

While the cattle grazed their fill, Little Wu sat dreaming of the money he would earn to help his family. It would be good to be more than a child and to take his part in making the family dream come true. How proud Baba and Mama would be of him! But there was still his private dream of the bracelet to wrestle with.

After a time, Old Ying told Little Wu to try driving all the cattle home without help. It took only a little running and shouting to get them all moving along the path.

"You can do the work well," said Old Ying. "I shall expect you to take them all out this evening."

Now Little Wu had another problem. Should he tell

Baba and Mama at once about his good fortune, or let them be surprised when they saw him taking out the herd? But he was too excited to keep still.

He found Mama busy pulling pickled radishes out of the big earthen brine jar for their morning meal. The special chopsticks she used for this were always hung on the wall away from the stove, where no grease could splatter on them, as the slightest trace of grease would cause the pickles to spoil. Thin rice was boiling in a black earthen pot, and slices of fresh bean cheese and chopped green onion were lying in a bowl ready to be fried.

"Quickly, Son," said Mama, "add a little fire and fan it for the frying. I see Baba coming."

She moved the rice pot aside and set the large round-bottomed iron cauldron over the fire hole of the small clay stove. Little Wu broke twigs from the neat pile by the wall and fed them into the stove, fanning vigorously to make the fire hot enough. Mama put a little lard into the cauldron and fried the cheese and onion.

"Mama," said Little Wu, as he wielded the woven bamboo fan, "Uncle Ying has asked me to drive his cattle to pasture for him. He will give me as much rice as I can carry at harvest time. He will also give me other work from time to time."

"That is very good," said Mama. "We have heard that Sister Ching is going to sell her small field this fall, and we are hoping that if we use every means in our power, we may have enough to buy it. Another load of rice will be a real help. I have been thinking, too, that since you are such a big boy now, we may be able to fatten two pigs this year, instead of one. You could bring food from the mountains for them. Do you think you can do that?"

Little Wu thought he could.

小吳與西瓜。

LITTLE WU did not know what he was doing. He only knew that Old Ying asked him to hoe a garden bed on a sunny slope. The hoe was heavy, with its stout wooden handle fitted into a hole in the long, sharp iron head that chopped deep into the ground. He hoed and hoed until the soil was as soft and smooth as cooked rice. Then Ying told him to make deep holes, put some rotted manure in each one, and cover it over with soil. Only when all was ready did Old Ying bring out the seeds they were to plant.

Such seeds! They looked like pumpkin seeds, except that they were small and black and hard.

"What are they?" Little Wu asked in wonder.

"Western melons," said Old Ying. "They are new here and not easy to grow. I got the seeds from Old Tai in Stone Village. He grew some last year to sell to the down-river people in the city, and he got a very good price for them. I paid him well for these few seeds."

Together they planted the seeds, placing three, point down, in each hole and firming the earth over them with their hands. When they had finished, there were two seeds left.

"Would you like to plant them somewhere for yourself?" asked Old Ying, not supposing that Little Wu could make the delicate plants grow.

"Thank you," murmured Little Wu, though he had no idea where he could find a place to plant them.

They spread a thin mulch of straw over the bed, and Old Ying explained that in their mountain climate the plants would have to be protected with straw every night until they were quite big.

With the seeds tucked in his pocket, Little Wu drove the cattle to pasture, stopping at his own house for Head One. He was wondering where he could plant his melons. The fields his father tended belonged to other men. The little space around his hut would be exposed to the hoofs of the cattle and the rooting of the pigs. There was no place.

While the cattle grazed, Little Wu scanned the mountainside. Up on the cliff, where few ever went, might there not be a pocket or two of earth? Swiftly he climbed, and soon found a rocky ledge a few feet long, with a little basin holding a pool of rain water. It was not hard to reach. As he would have to come every day with the cattle, no one would notice his frequent visits.

Staring at the scanty soil, he made a plan.

Hour after hour he toiled, that day and the next, dragging stones to rim the ledge and scraping old manure and earth from here and there to fill in a little terrace, facing the south. It was hard work for a ten-year-old, and his muscles ached as at last he tucked the two precious seeds into the soft soil and spread dry grass from the mountain over the top. The spring sunshine reflected down from the cliff and warmed the seed bed. Every day Little Wu carried water from a near-by spring and peered under the grass to look for seedlings. In a few days they came, green and sturdy, a delight to his heart.

The spring sunshine was soft and warm. Orange, plum, and peach blossoms had fallen long ago. Here and there the dark, shining green of pomegranate trees was splashed with the amazing red of their blossoms. *"Shih-liu hua"* Little Wu called them, and he loved to climb the trees and bring down a bright flower or two. One day, while he was up in a tree picking flowers, a Chinese woman with a sweet, homely face stopped to watch him. She was holding a little girl with fair skin.

"I want *shih-liu hua,*" said the child.

"Please throw us one or two," said the woman.

He tossed down what he had, and the nursemaid tucked them into the hair of the little one.

"Beautiful?" asked the girl.

"Now you are really beautiful," the woman replied.

That gave Little Wu an idea. He gathered some more flowers and ran home to his mother.

"Mama," he said, "guess what I have brought you."

"Some mushrooms?"

"No."

"Some eels?" Mama guessed.

"No." Little Wu shook his head, smiling.

"A rabbit?"

"No, nothing like that."

"Then how can I guess?"

"Flowers to put in your hair. Sit down, and I will put them on you."

She sat down, while he tried the flowers this way and that, deciding that he liked them best behind her ears. He tucked the stems into her hair.

"That's really beautiful," he said. "Will you wear them all day?"

"No," she replied, "only for you, here in the house. Flowers in the hair are for little girls, not for grown-ups. Everybody would laugh at me."

So that's it, thought Little Wu. Women can wear only jewelry, not flowers. Well, she shall have jewelry to wear if the melons grow.

Spring days were busy days. Old Ying's buffalo were working early and late plowing the fields, and had to be pastured whenever the men stopped to eat and rest. More and more, Little Wu began to take part in the work that had to be done. While Baba was out plowing a seedbed Little Wu learned to swing the heavy mallet to make *ba*.

Ba was the common food of his tribe. It was made by steaming glutinous rice and some coarse grain like sorghum seeds or the seeds of rice weeds and pounding them together in a big wooden trough until they were a smooth, thick dough. This was formed into round cakes and allowed to harden. Slices of it, when toasted, became crisp outside and soft inside, good to fill a hungry little boy.

It was hard work, lifting the heavy mallet and letting it fall. Mama took turns when Little Wu's breath came hard. There was no time to waste, for the mass would harden as it cooled. Before it was too cold to work, every grain must be mashed well. Thump, thump, thump! Muscles aching, breath puffing, pound the *ba,* pound the *ba!* Then form it into cakes and set it away!

When no one was looking, Little Wu liked to pull aside the cloth cover and admire the *ba* that he had made. To him it tasted better than anything. He liked to toast a slice or two and eat it before going out to look at his melon seedlings.

小吳與西瓜。

"MARKET TODAY," said Baba, early one fine morning. "I am going to buy our two little pigs. Who wants to go with me?"

"I do!" shouted Little Wu.

"Hop on my shoulders, then, and get the pig baskets down."

Baba swung the boy up so that he could untie the two long baskets from the rafters and drop them to the ground. They were open at one end, just big enough to hold a pig of market age.

"Aren't you two lucky!" said Mama. "I will sit there selling my cheese as usual, while over in the cattle market you are bargaining for the finest young pigs in Flowery River. I will not sell the bean residue today, because we shall need it for our piggies."

She was busy as she spoke, grinding in a little stone hand mill the wet soybeans she had put to soak the day before. A milky fluid ran out as she ground. When she was done, she strained the mash through a cloth, brought the milk to a boil, and set it aside. She then took part of the residue and set it to cook with onion and winter radish for the family breakfast.

When Little Wu came back from pasture, she served him a bowl of the fresh bean milk, followed by a bowl of the bean and vegetable mixture—strong food for a boy with a big day ahead of him. Two slices of toasted *ba* completed the meal.

By this time Mama had curdled the bean milk and poured it into wooden moulds, marked in squares on the bottom. The whey was draining off, as the cheese hardened to a quivery texture. While it was setting, Mama carefully washed all the utensils she had used with hot water. They had to be kept perfectly clean, or the milk and cheese would have a strong taste. Little Wu helped her, chatting of pigs all the while.

"They will grow so big," he said, "that Baba will have to build a new sty."

"And you will run so far getting greens for them that your legs will get as hard as branches of trees. Then, when Baba builds the new sty, he will make a mistake and use your legs for the framework."

"If he does," said Little Wu, "the sty will run away and hide, and take the pigs with it."

They laughed at their nonsense. Then Baba came in

from the fields and washed himself, and they all put on clean trousers and jackets. It was time to go.

Market days were always a treat. People would go to market even if they had nothing to buy or sell, just to meet their friends, hear the latest gossip, and enjoy the sights and sounds and smells.

The market place was like a great X. In the middle were fruit, cakes, and sweetmeats, and sometimes a story teller or magician. To the west were vendors of earthenware, baskets, and furniture; to the east, vegetables, poultry, fish, and meat; to the north, cloth, raw hemp, and embroidery thread; and to the south, medicines, dyestuffs, sulphur, and other odds and ends.

The vendors would begin to gather by the middle of the morning, choosing the best spots to spread their wares out on the ground or on trestle tables. By noon the market would be in full swing, and it was a very colorful sight. Baskets of bright fruit, vegetables, and flowers could be seen sometimes from more than a mile away, as their owners came striding down the mountain paths in single file on their way to market.

The gayest costumes belonged to the women of Little Wu's tribe, with accordion-pleated blue hemp cloth kilts swinging around their knees and jackets covered thickly with bright cross-stitch designs. The Blue Miao, from several miles away, were very interesting too, with nothing but blue and white in their costumes.

Then there were the Chung Chia, who spoke a different language, although it didn't matter, since everyone, no matter what tribe he belonged to, could speak Chinese. They were tall, with fair skin and pink cheeks. The women wore their long black hair in braids around their heads and dressed in an ancient Chinese style, with many rows of fine embroidery around their shoulders and the lower part of their wide trousers.

The Chinese traders and restaurant keepers from the city, who came by pony cart and carried away loads of produce, seemed very dull in their dark blue or gray clothing, as did also the down-river people. Only here and there would be seen a rich woman from the city in a bright silk gown.

Away from the main market place, where the road sloped down to the river, was the livestock market. Little Wu always loved any excuse to go there and watch the animals. There were huge buffalo, their horns polished with soot and lard and their hides powdery with white lime. There were buffalo calves, too big to drink milk, but still wanting it and being pushed away by their mothers' big curved horns. There were ponderous billy goats, fit for the funeral feast of a Confucian scholar, dainty nanny goats, and lovable, capering kids. There were pack ponies, with saddle marks on their backs and fluffy red tassels on their halters. There were yellow cows, with huge, soft eyes, and sometimes a cat, or a litter of puppies, or even a monkey. And in the spring there were little pigs, packed in baskets, ready to be bought and fattened.

Baba walked up and down, examining the pigs and

listening to the haggling that was going on between owners and buyers. When he had an idea of the prices that were being paid, he approached a man whose piglets were plump and lively.

"How much for these two little pigs?" he asked.

"Oh, these are fine pigs," said the man, "but I will sell them cheap." He named his price, about double what he expected to receive.

Baba snorted and turned away, naming a price about half what he was willing to pay. The vendor quickly reduced his figure a little, Baba turned back, and they settled down to the serious business of agreeing on a price. Little Wu stood by, trying not to show how much he admired and longed for the black piglet with the pink nose and the one with the white spot on its back. If the vendor saw that he had set his heart on those, Baba might have to pay more. At last the bargain was made, and Little Wu was allowed to carry the pigs in two baskets slung from the ends of a shoulder pole.

They went first to find Mama. "Look," cried Little
Wu, "aren't they beauties? I'm going to call this one Small
Black and that one Small Spot."

"They certainly are fine," Mama agreed. "If we can't

raise them to a big size, I'm much mistaken. They will put many dollars in the gourd."

"Will you be ready to go home soon? The pigs must be hungry. See how they wiggle their snouts."

"I still have several squares of cheese to sell. But it should not take long."

"Shan't I carry the pigs?" asked Baba as they started for home.

"No, I want to," replied Little Wu.

Baba picked up the empty cheese trays. As they walked along, Little Wu told Mama he wanted to care for the pigs.

"You will have to wash the old feeding tub that stands behind the house. Then you may take part of the bean residue and mix it with water for the pigs. When you have put them in the sty, you may take a wrapping cloth and go to the mountainside to bring home green things for them. You must bring only plants that you know."

When they reached home, Baba went to work in the fields, and Little Wu fed the pigs.

After that, the days were fuller than ever. Every time he pastured the cattle, Little Wu carried water in an old crock to his terrace, where the melon seedlings stood green and strong. Then he foraged farther and farther into the mountains for pig food, as the growing animals needed more and more. When the plants flowered and the little melons began to grow, he trained the spreading vines over the rocks where he could reach them and carried armfuls of grass to make a soft cushion for each melon to lie on. It was his greatest joy to see the smooth, green fruit swelling bigger and bigger and to think how pleased his mother would be when he bought her a shiny bracelet to wear.

Often other boys took their cattle to the same grazing grounds as Little Wu. He always tried to get there earlier or stay later than the others, so that he could visit his melons unobserved. The terrace was on the other side of a spur of rock from where the children played, but they would notice if Little Wu wandered away from their games every day.

They had wonderful times together. They ran races and
turned somersaults and kicked shuttlecocks. The older ones
would tell ghost stories. Some of them had bamboo flutes

only a few inches long and were learning to play the wild, wailing cadences of their tribal music. One day they almost caught a small deerlike animal with long tusks that had ventured out of the hills to drink at the spring.

More and more often, Old Ying would ask Little Wu to help him, as he found the boy quick and willing. There were weeding and hoeing to do, errands to run, and the three ducks to bring home when they strayed. Each time there would be a little money or a little food to take home.

One day he came home late and wet.

"Mama," he said. "I had such trouble! The magistrate's big foreign dog ran right into Uncle Chu's rice field to chase Uncle Ying's ducks, and the ducks were so frightened they wouldn't come out of the water afterward. I had to go in after them."

"Go change your clothes," said Mama. "I was late myself, and the meal isn't ready yet. Chen Lady asked me to weed her garden, because her helper was sick. When Feng Lady saw me working, she asked me to do her garden too, every week from now on. That will bring in a good bit of money."

"I had good luck today too," said Baba. "This afternoon Sister Chu came to tell me that Old Chu has gone away to hide from the malaria demon that has been bothering him. Somebody must drive his pony cart to Kweiyang for a few days. She will give me half of what I bring back, after paying for the pony's feed. I really begin to think that we may be able to buy Sister Ching's field."

"Baba!" Little Wu was excited. "Do you suppose I could ride with you? I have never been to Kweiyang."

"That would be nice," said Baba, "but who would take care of the buffalo that day? Besides, you would take room in the cart where there might be a paying passenger. It takes three hours to go to Kweiyang, and the pony must rest and be fed before returning. Then I may have to wait an hour or two for passengers. When you are a little older, we will take you to Kweiyang for the dance festival, but this time you had better stay home."

Little Wu swallowed his disappointment. Every morning he went with Baba to feed and brush the pony and hitch it to the cart. Every evening, near sunset, when Baba returned with a handful of money, they fed the pony and examined its feet for stones.

The gourd became so full of money that they buried it in a corner of the floor and started to fill another one. They allowed themselves to speak more and more often of Sister Ching's field, which after all was a very little one. The load of rice Little Wu would get at harvest time and the price of the fattened pigs would go far to put them within reach of their goal.

AT FIRST it didn't seem too important that several days passed without rain. Then Little Wu began to notice groups of men walking among the rice fields, poking sticks into the water to see how deep it was, and shaking their heads. Soon he realized that for a long time he had not seen even a little cloud. The hot sun and the dry wind drew the water out of the earth. Uncle and

小吳與西瓜

Auntie Lin, who had land beside the river, were working long hours, swinging a wooden bucket on a rope between them, lifting water into their field. Another field was kept full by an old water wheel which was turned by the current of the river. The wheel had hollow sections of bamboo fixed to it, and as each one reached the top, it would spill its water into a bamboo trough which carried it where it was needed.

But most land was too high and too far from the river to be helped. Even if a man spent all his time carrying pails of water, it would not be enough.

The spring on the mountainside from which Little Wu carried water to his melons was still running. He had only to carry more than before. He also carried many armloads of grass to spread over the terrace, to keep the precious water from being sucked out of the ground by the thirsty sun.

One evening Baba reported that he had gone with a group to consult Chang the Wise Man, an old Confucian

scholar, about what to do. They had suggested that he ask the magistrate to stop all slaughtering of animals for three days. Chang had answered that the magistrate was a modern-minded man, who would think such actions superstitious. If they wanted to appease Heaven, they would have to do it without official help.

They had then sent a group to talk to the butchers' guild, asking them to give up three days' profit for the good of all.

"Remember," they said, "if the crops fail and there is a famine, you will suffer as much as we do. Is it not better to make some sacrifice now, to please Heaven and avoid the trouble?"

The butchers agreed, and for three days no blood was shed in Flowery River.

Every evening the moon shone brightly, and a group of young men sat up late playing their little flutes. Little Wu liked to lie awake as long as he could, listening to the wild, echoing music which rose and fell, wailed, died away, and rose again, until it mingled with his dreams.

More and more often those dreams were of being hungry, as his parents' fear spread to his own mind; and Mama began to skimp on food to make what they had last a long time. He heard Baba and others tell about the famine they had lived through in their youth and how many people had died.

Men brought out the great rain dragon made of cloth stretched over a bamboo frame, and organized a procession. The dragon was carried along the streets, followed by men beating drums and gongs. Pails of water were poured over it to remind it to do its duty.

But the sun still shone as hot as ever. At last the ground was quite dry in the fields. The rice plants looked dull and soft. The village elders met in solemn council and then made an announcement to the people.

"Our only hope," they said, "is in Heaven Father. The children must pray for rain. As they are the ones who least deserve to suffer, Heaven Father will surely listen to them."

In the evening, all the children met in front of the village shrine. Tea, rice, and incense were offered to the gods. Then each child was given a stick of lighted incense that gave off a fragrant smoke.

An older boy who had already memorized the prayer they were to use led the procession. He shouted a line of the prayer, and all the children repeated it after him, rais-

ing their incense high in the air as they did so. They marched along the narrow paths, twisting among the fields, from one end of the village land to the other. In the darkness, the glowing tips of the incense looked to Little Wu like an army of fireflies. He loved the sight and the sweet smell. He loved the words they chanted. Most of all, he

liked to think that Heaven Father would hear and see and smell, and would love the children and send rain to give them food. It made him feel very important to take part in such a serious and beautiful ceremony.

Over and over they chanted:

Ch'ing T'ien, Ch'ing T'ien!
Pei hsing k'e lien!
Lao T'ien hsia yü
Hao ta yang t'ien!
Ta yü lo tsai t'ien chung chien,
Hsiao yü lo tsai hou t'sai yuan!

Blue Sky, Blue Sky!
Pity the people!
Old Heaven send rain
To feed the crops!
Big rain to run into the rice field;
Small rain for the back vegetable garden!

For five nights the ceremony was repeated. Little Wu was getting sleepy because it kept him up late. He wondered how much longer it would go on. On the sixth day things seemed very bad. Great cracks had opened in the dry earth of the fields, and the plants were drooping.

As he rode Head One out to pasture he looked sadly at the land. He closed his eyes and thought, "Heaven Father, our need is great. We have no hope but in you."

While the buffalo were grazing, he noticed that the wind, which had blown steadily down the valley from the south for so long, was shifting. He remembered the weather saying that he had often heard:

> *South wind, hot sun;*
> *North wind, big rain;*
> *West wind, fine weather;*
> *East wind, cold, wet.*

"North wind, come! North wind, come!" he said over and over.

As he rode home, the wind was at his back, roaring up the valley, a north wind indeed! Great black clouds came boiling over the mountains.

When he reached home, Mama told him to run and find the pigs, which had gone out to forage in the woods. He ran along the path, calling, "Oooh, lu-lu-lu-lu-lu! Oooh, lu-lu-lu-lu-lu!" They were nowhere to be seen.

The heavy clouds were all over the sky now, except for a copper-colored streak in the east. It was so dark that it would be hard to find a frightened little pig in the thickets. Little Wu was frightened, too. He ran back and forth, pulling back low branches and calling the pigs. There was a flash of lightning so great that for a moment Little Wu thought Heaven itself had opened around him. The whole earth was shaken by the thunder. Great drops of rain rattled on the leaves, and then came a rush of water as if the thunder had opened the sluicegates of the Heavenly River.

Little Wu stood bewildered. He wanted to run to his melon patch, where such a rain might wash all the soil away. He wanted to run home, where Mama would make a good fire to dry his clothes. But he had to find the pigs, and how could he? Just as he was ready to cry, another flash of lightning showed him a little pink nose under a low bush not five feet away.

He plunged forward, groped under the leaves, and pulled out the two pigs, which were huddled together, soaking wet. With his stick, he sent them scampering homeward. He followed them, slipping in the mud of the path. On the way he met Baba coming out to look for him.

"Baba," gasped Little Wu, "please take the pigs home. I have something else to do."

"What can you have to do in this weather except get in the house, little dullwit?"

"Uncle Ying has given me something to do," said Little Wu, and, thrusting the stick into Baba's hand, he turned and ran back through the woods.

He wasn't sure he liked having said that. He had been worrying about what excuse he could make for staying out, without giving away his secret. But the words seemed to come out naturally, and as he thought it over, he decided it was true enough. Had not Old Ying given him the seeds?

Running as much as he could, he soon came to the melon patch. Just as he had feared, the water was spouting down from the cliff onto the little terrace that he had built with so much work. The dry grass had floated aside, and the soil was being washed from the roots of melon vines.

Seizing the earthen bowl which he kept hidden behind a rock, Little Wu held it to catch the spouting stream of water. When it was full he emptied it and returned for more. Meanwhile, with his bare feet, he pulled back the piles of grass and rearranged them around the plants to protect the soil.

It rained as if it would never stop. Far away, among the fields, men shouted joyfully to each other as they moved about, opening or closing the irrigation channels to direct the water where it was needed. At last all was quiet. The

village slept, in preparation for the busy day to come. Still
Little Wu stood with his bowl, tossing the water away from
his melon bed. A good smell arose from the wet earth and
a good feeling covered the land as the thirsty plants drank

of the water and stretched out their wilted leaves, crisp and strong again.

When at last the rain stopped, Little Wu started home, wiggling his toes to make the mud squish through them. He was wondering what he should say to Mama and whether she would be angry with him for staying out so long. As he drew near the house, his feet dragged, and he felt suddenly very tired. If only he could be safe and dry in bed, without having to speak to anyone!

But there was Mama sitting in the doorway, her fingers busy twisting hemp, winding the fibers smoothly in the dark as she waited for her little boy.

"How do you happen to come so late?" she asked, and her soft voice was as near to anger as Little Wu had ever heard it.

"Right does not dwell with me," said Little Wu, using the common form of apology. "I had to take care of the melon patch, where the rain was washing the soil away. I hoped you would not worry about me."

He was glad he had told the truth, but feared he would have to say whose melon patch it had been.

Mama patted his wet head. "I am sorry," she said. "I forgot that you are like a big boy now, although you are so young. I should have known that you had a good reason for what you did, but I could think of no good reason for such a little boy to stay out so long. Now quickly change your wet clothes and drink this hot gruel before you go to bed."

The hot rice gruel took the shivery feeling out of Little Wu's bones. When he crawled into his quilt he found that Mama had even heated a stone in the fire and wrapped it in old cloths to warm his feet. What a mother she was! Third Wang's mother would surely have wakened the neighbors with her scolding in such a case.

As he drifted off to sleep, he seemed to see his mother in the market place, wearing so many silver neck rings that her chin was forced up in the air, like Second Lin's bride at the betrothal feast, silver chopsticks thrust through her hair, and her arms weighed down with delicate bracelets. Nothing was too good for her! Little Wu dreamed that he was holding her hand, proud to be seen as the son of the most beautiful mother in the world.

THE MELONS grew and grew, dark green and smooth. Little Wu took what chances he could to ask questions about them, until, seeing his interest, Old Ying gave him the job of watching for them to get ripe. Every day he was to tap the largest ones. When they gave a hollow sound they would be ready for market.

小吳與西瓜

He tapped his own melons too. Warmed by the sun from the cliff and watered regularly all through the drought, they were ahead of Old Ying's. The day came soon when two of the largest gave a deep hollow sound to his tapping. Then Little Wu did not know what to do. How could he be the first to sell western melons? How could he know what price to ask? What would Old Ying think, if Little Wu spoiled the market by getting there first and charging too little? There was only one thing he could do. When he brought the cattle home that evening, he went to Old Ying, who was busy making a turnip seedbed.

"Uncle," he said, "do you remember the two seeds you gave me when we planted the western melons?"

"Yes," said Old Ying. "What did you do with them?"

"I planted them on the hot mountainside near where I pasture the cattle, and now they are ripe, and I don't know how to sell them, or whether you will be angry if I sell mine before yours."

"You say they are already ripe?"

"Yes, two of them make a hollow sound when I tap them."

"That is amazing. I will go with you to see them."

Together they walked through the fields to the pasture and climbed the cliff to the terrace. On the way, Little Wu told how he had kept the melons secret from his parents in order to buy a gift for his mother and asked Old Ying to keep quiet about it. Old Ying promised, smiling. In his mind, too, nothing was too good for Little Wu's mother.

Old Ying stared at the thick, leafy vines and the smooth, dark melons. Then he knelt among the rocks and tapped them.

"Yes," he said, "these two are ripe. I never would have believed it. When I gave you the seeds, I did not think you could make them grow. It is not easy in our mountain climate. I have taken great care of my own patch, and still they are not like these."

"What shall I do?" asked Little Wu.

"You must take them to market tomorrow. I will ask

Old Tai of Stone Village what the price should be, since he and I are the only ones who will have them for sale. You must ask a high price, which down-river people will pay because they have not seen these melons for a long time.

You must not sell them cheap, because it would spoil the market for those coming later, Tai's and mine. Keep your price high, and I will come when I finish selling my buffalo calf, to see how it is going. If you have still not sold them, I will help you."

The next day, when it was time to start for market, Little Wu had not finished feeding the pigs. He told Baba and Mama to go first; he would take care of himself. When they were gone, he ran to the terrace, put his two melons in a sack, and went trudging to the cattle market to find Old Ying.

"Has Old Tai told you the price?" he asked.

Old Ying bent down and whispered his instructions. Little Wu nodded and went to find a place in the vegetable market, as far as possible from where his mother had set her trays of bean cheese. Laying the melons neatly on top of the folded sack, he sat down behind them.

Many people glanced curiously at the melons, and some asked what they were. Very few asked the price, and those who did cried out in horror and walked on. Little Wu was not too much discouraged, since he knew that Old Ying would come to help him, but it did get very dull, sitting there with nothing to do but look hopefully at people.

An old man near by had a fine catch of fish in covered tubs of water. It was fun to watch the large, shiny fish wiggle and flash in the sun as they were sold. Little Wu became so much interested in watching that he had almost forgotten his business, when suddenly a tall man and woman in down-river clothes gave a cry of joy.

"Western melons, you look!"

"How much money?" asked the man.

Little Wu named his price in a firm voice, as if it were a settled matter. The two spoke together softly, then examined and tapped the melons. They offered a price far below what Little Wu had asked.

"There is no reduction," said Little Wu, stiffly. "These western melons are the first of the season, and the finest you will see. They are a rarity here, and many people are eager to gain face by serving them to their friends."

After whispering together, the couple named a price only slightly below what Little Wu had asked. He agreed, grumbling a little, as was the custom in the market, and one melon was sold.

The bills left in Little Wu's hands were crisp and new. They were more money than he had ever touched in his life. Quickly he folded them and tucked them far down in his pocket. Then he looked at the crowd with new interest. To think that there were really people who could spend all that good money for a melon! He looked at the few down-river people who came by, wondering how much they had in their pockets. As a pretty Chinese woman in a gray silk gown passed him, he called out:

"Western melon! The first of the season! How long since you have seen a western melon?"

The woman turned quickly, examined the melon, and bought it at a good price, uttering soft cries of pleasure as she did so. Her manservant put the melon in his basket,

grumbling that there would be no room for the other things they must buy.

Little Wu tucked the money into his pocket and ran to the cattle market to report to Old Ying, who praised him for his success. Then he went to find Mama and ask if she had anything for him to do.

Since she had no errand for him, he wandered to the center of the market place and walked up and down among the vendors of jewelry, looking, listening, and learning. The money he had was many times more than enough for a brass bracelet. It would be enough for a thin silver bracelet or a stout silver hairpin. As he thought about really buying such a thing, now that he had the means, he hesitated. Would Mama be pleased to have such a gift, when the field was her one dream? If the money were her own, she would choose to save it. Might she not even scold him? Much as he longed to see her wear an ornament, he dared not buy it yet. Perhaps after the question of the field was settled would be a better time.

So he went back to find Old Ying and asked his help in turning the paper money into silver, which would be safe to keep until fall.

Twice more, as the melons ripened, Little Wu carried them to market and sold them. At last there was left only the one he meant to save for seed. Old Ying told him he would not have to waste a melon this way, as his own would give more than enough seeds for them both, and so the last melon was sold too. Of course the price was not so high as for the first ones, but still higher than for other fruits. Little Wu took an old scrap of cloth and tied the money around his waist, where he could feel it as he ran about by day and lay in bed at night.

It was far too much for a bracelet, even a silver one. Maybe he could get a silver neck ring! He was almost frightened at the thought of spending so much money. He would visit the jewelry stands as often as he could, to learn things, and in the fall, after the field was bought, he would know better what to do.

THEN IT WAS harvest time, and everyone was too busy to think of anything but the work and the weather. The banks of the fields had been broken to drain the water off and permit the rice to ripen. Now it stood, golden in the sunshine, the heads bent over with the weight of the good grain.

A schedule was drawn up for the exchange of work

小吳與西瓜

among neighbor families, as harvesting was too big a job
for any family to do alone. Baba and Old Ying were on the
same team. They sharpened sickles and cleaned the great
threshing box. The women swept the storage bins and the
stone-paved courtyards where the grain would be spread to
dry in the sun.

At last it was time to begin. The weather was clear
and warm. After the morning chores and breakfast were
done, six families gathered together, at a different home each

day. The man whose crop was to be cut had to provide a feast for the workers, with a variety of vegetable dishes, meat, and wine.

The men went off to prepare for the day's work, moving the threshing box into the field, laying sacks and baskets ready, and whetting their sickles to a razor edge so that they would cut smoothly, with no jerk to shake the rice out of the heads.

Meanwhile the women made preparations for the feast.

They set up a long table of bed boards set on sawhorses in front of the house, for no home was big enough to hold such a party inside. They prepared vegetables and meat and several kinds of dried bean cheese for cooking. Then, leaving a few women to do the rest, they joined the men in the fields.

Women and older boys cut the long, gleaming armfuls of rice plants and laid them in piles on the warm ground. Men picked up the piles and carried them to the huge wooden box with sloping sides. Holding the stems, they slammed the grain-laden heads against the sides of the box, so that the rice, in its yellow husks, fell inside. Little Wu and the other small boys and girls gathered up the stalks that were missed or dropped. The clean straw grew into a great pile, and the box slowly filled with bushels of grain, which finally had to be put into baskets and sacks and carried away to make room for more.

It was a good harvest. The drought had not lasted long enough to hurt the crop very much. The grains were

plump in the well-filled heads. Everyone was filled with joy
and thankfulness at the sight.

The women in the kitchen had a busy time, tending the fire under the huge rice steamer and the little charcoal pots over which great chunks of fat pork were simmering. They ground quantities of dry red peppers into powder, for a meal is not a meal to a Miao without plenty of hot pepper. Since it was a feast day, there was also hard rock salt to be pulverized. Mountains of green vegetables were washed and cut up, and bean milk was made into fresh, tender curds and whey. Kernels of unripe corn were ground, formed into flat cakes, wrapped in leaves, and steamed.

Long before time for the feast, children began to hang around the kitchen, attracted by the wonderful odors. The busy women had no time for them.

"Go outside to play," they would scold, slipping a bit of corn cake into each little hand.

It was hard to go out when things smelled so good. Meat was so rare a treat that most of them never tasted it except on special occasions. Even now, they might get little more than a taste. The feast, after all, was for the men.

The women and children would share what was left. Food there would be for all, but the best dishes might be finished at the men's table.

After the meal, everyone lay down on the warm earth to rest for a while. How good it felt to let their tired bodies relax and to feel new strength flowing into them from the good food they had eaten! Some slept, some joked, and some just lay looking at the sky and the hills and the golden fields. Then the rest period was over, and the work went on until the last grain of rice was stored.

On the day when Old Ying's fields were done, Little Wu was beside himself with excitement, for this was the day when he would collect his pay for pasturing the buffalo. He dared give no sign that he expected anything, but he kept watching for what Old Ying would do.

When it was time to start carrying the rice to the store room, Old Ying personally chose two baskets and a light shoulder pole, telling Little Wu to stand ready. The baskets were half filled with rice, and Little Wu put his shoulders to the pole. He stood up easily, with the baskets swinging.

Someone shouted, "He can carry more than that!" More rice was added, and more and more, while the men stood in a circle, cheering. At last Little Wu could just get the baskets off the ground. He staggered a few steps and put them down.

"Is it too much?" asked his father.

"No, I can do it," puffed Little Wu.

Amid shouts of encouragement, he again set his shoulder to the pole and moved forward. Little by little, stopping every few steps, he moved to the edge of the field. As he stood gathering his strength for the climb up the bank, Old Ying called to Baba:

"You take it home now. He has proved that he can carry it."

Baba ran over, lifted the load, and swung along toward home, an excited Little Wu running by his side. As they neared the house, he told Little Wu to take it again, while

he went ahead to tell Mama, who had gone home to feed the pigs.

Tears rose to Mama's eyes as she stood in the doorway and saw her little boy staggering toward her under his precious load. She ran out to meet him, put her arm around his shoulders, and said:

"What a boy! It is like having two men in the house!"

When the harvest was over, Sister Ching was ready to sell her field. Baba and Mama thought over how much money they had in the gourds. Little Wu's rice was sold, together with what they could spare of Baba's crop. If only the pigs were full-grown, they could be sold for enough to make up the amount needed. It would be a pity to sell them so young, when the money they would bring might not be enough.

Baba and Little Wu went to Sister Ching to bargain for the field.

"I can pay you most of the money now, and the rest when the pigs are grown," Baba said.

"That won't do, Brother Wu," she replied. "Old Huang has offered me a good price at once. For friendship's sake, I would like to let you have the field, but one's own chicken is worth more than another's pig. I will give you just three days to meet Old Huang's price. That will be market day, so you will have a fair chance to raise the money if you can find a way."

"Thank you, Sister," said Baba, and walked home, thinking hard. Little Wu trotted beside him, thinking too. There must be something they could do, some way to raise a few dollars. But no, they had been thinking all summer, and had left no stone unturned to make money. What could

they do in three days? Make sandals and mattresses? Have Mama boil and sell her last lot of hemp thread? Get some lucky odd job? Any or all of these they could and would do, but it would not be enough.

Little Wu sat in the doorway listening, as Baba and Mama discussed the matter. They cracked the gourds and counted the money, thinking they might be wrong about how much they had.

"There is still Old Wang, the moneylender," said Baba.

"You know better than that," Mama protested. "You know people who borrow from him must pay such high interest that they can never get the principal paid back, and they are lucky if they do not lose everything they have to him."

"You are right," said Baba; "it is not to be thought of. But there must be some way, when we are so near."

Little Wu thought of the money tied around his waist. He thought of the present he wanted to buy his mother. Still thinking, he went out to take the buffalo to pasture.

HIS MONEY would make up what was needed to buy the field, but how could he bear to give it up? How could he ever find another way to make money secretly?

The rocking gait of Head One at last brought a new thought into his mind. He remembered how they had bought the little beast nearly two years before, and how every plan in the family since then had been directed toward having a field to plow when the buffalo was big enough to do it. Suddenly he remembered how one day in the market place Mama had watched Third Wang's mother, in her finery, flirting with the men who bought her onion cakes, and she had said:

"Silly little one! She will always be poor. There is no help for a person like that."

Now Mama's big dream was within her grasp, thanks to Little Wu's little dream. All at once he knew that the bracelet had been a very little dream indeed. He had wanted his wise, beautiful mother to be something she wasn't.

As soon as the buffalo had grazed their fill, he started them homeward. Never had Head One's steps seemed so slow to an impatient little boy.

At home, the meal was ready. Little Wu rushed to the table and said:

"Baba and Mama, I have a surprise for you, but it is a long story, and I want you to listen until it is done."

His parents, thinking he might have dug some eels or caught a pheasant, promised to listen quietly. Never had they dreamed of such a story as the one he told. When at last he took the money from his waist and laid it before them, they were speechless with amazement and joy.

"Very good, very good," said Baba at last. "I will sell the pigs tomorrow, and the field will be ours. It is a good end for a hard summer. We can plant horsebeans for winter, and they will all be our own."

Mama put down her chopsticks and hugged Little Wu.

"I am very happy that you wanted to buy me an ornament," she said, "but I am still more pleased that you were wise enough to change your mind. Many women may have ornaments, but very few can have a son like you."

The next day was a busy one. Baba took the pigs to market early. Mama polished the silver dollars, counting them lovingly, as she remembered all the ways they had earned them. Then, while Mama went to market with her bean cheese, Baba and Little Wu went to see Sister Ching and arranged to meet her in the tea house near the market.

They asked Old Ying to go with them as one of the witnesses. For the other, they hoped to find someone who could write well enough to draw up the deed.

"There's Old Tai," said Ying, as they crossed the market place. "He will do."

Tai agreed. The men sat down in the tea house, and

Sister Ching soon joined them. The new deed was written, giving the Wu family title to "earth and sky," and with "Land and Money All Clear" in large characters. Sister Ching and the witnesses moistened their seals on pads of vermillion and pressed them on the thin, tough paper. Baba, who could not write and had no seal, made a thumb print under his name. The money was counted out, and the old deed given up.

Returning to the market, Baba and Little Wu walked around to approach Mama from behind, while Old Tai went up to her with the deed in his hand.

"A letter has come for you, Elder Sister-in-Law," he said respectfully.

"A letter? Who would write me a letter? I can't read!" she protested.

"I will read it to you," he replied. " 'Hereby Ching Mei-chen, with the consent of her children, willingly transfers the title to the following land . . .' "

Mama was so happy that she did not hear the rest

clearly. Baba and Little Wu crept out from behind her, and
the boy took the hands of his parents, jumping up and
down with joy. What a wonderful feeling it was! Look-

ing up, he was puzzled to see a tear running down Mama's nose.

Baba gave Little Wu some money to buy himself a treat. Excited beyond words at having money to spend as he pleased, the boy ran off to the center of the market where peanuts and sweetmeats were displayed. As soon as he was gone, Baba whispered to Mama and put something into her hand, which she quickly tucked into her pocket.

Then Little Wu was back, offering his parents some of his peanut candy. Mama said to Baba:

"Please watch the cheese for a little while. I want the boy to go with me to carry something."

Together they walked again to the center of the market, and turned to the right. To Little Wu's surprise, they stopped at a jewelry stand.

"I want you to choose something for me," said Mama. "We had a little more money than we needed for the field, and so Baba said you should have your wish too. We have enough to buy a silver hairpin if we bargain well, and I shall wear it with pride, thinking how you wanted me to have it."

Little Wu did not know any word for the kind of happiness that filled him as he looked at the hairpins. He chose one with an oval head that reminded him of his melon seeds. When Mama had paid for it and thrust it through her hair, he took her hand and looked up at her, remembering his dream.

Then he looked around the market, wondering that no one stopped to stare at her. Couldn't they see that she was the most beautiful mother in the world?